Friends Are Forever

Yummy
Ice-Cream

Written by Emma Quay

Illustrated by Anna Walker

SCHOLASTIC

For you, Dad ~ EQ

For Charlie and Henry ~ AW

First published in 2009 by Scholastic Australia

This edition first published in 2010 by Scholastic Children's Books

Euston House, 24 Eversholt Street

London NWI IDB

a division of Scholastic Ltd

www.scholastic.co.uk

London ~ New York ~ Toronto ~ Sydney ~ Auckland

Mexico City ~ New Delhi ~ Hong Kong

www.emmaquay.com

www.annawalker.com.au

ISBN 978 1407 12067 6

Hello, Panda.

Hello, Sheep.

Hello, Owl.

All together . . . friends are forever.

Sheep and Panda
have ice-creams.

"Yummy ice-cream,"
says Panda.

"It looks yummy,"
says Owl.

"Really yummy ice-cream,"
says Sheep.

"It looks
really yummy,"
says Owl.

Panda's ice-cream
is chocolate.

Sheep's ice-cream
is strawberry.

Owl's eyes are big and round.

Panda and Sheep
break off the pointy
ends of their cones . . .

and scoop up little dollops
of ice-cream.

"Very yummy ice-creams!"
says Owl.

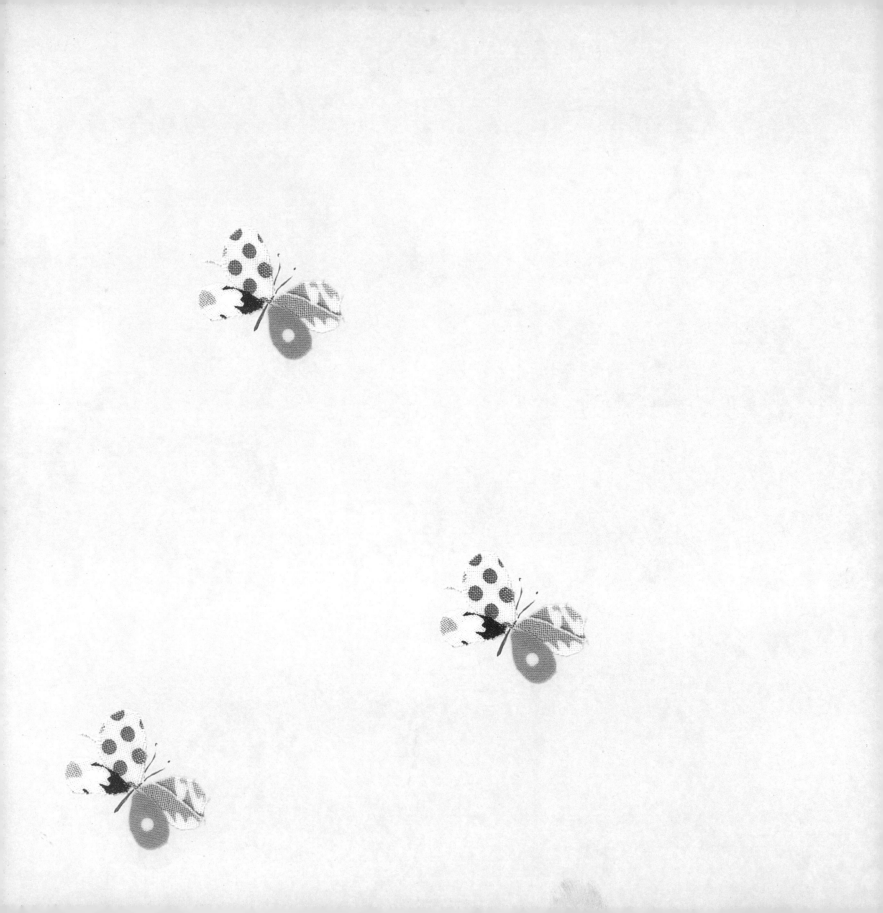